Secret PRINCESSES

Sea Turtle Song

ROSIE BANKS

Wishing Star Palace

The Secret Princess Promise

"I promise that I will be kind and brave,

Using my magic to help and save,

Granting wishes and doing my best,

To make people smile and bring happiness."

CONTENTS

CHAPTER ONE
Painting Party

"I've been dying to come here!" said Mia Thompson excitedly. A bell tinkled as she opened the door and stepped inside the Ceramics Café with a group of her friends from school.

It was her friend Connie's birthday, and Connie's mum had taken the girls to paint pottery at a new place that had just

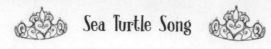
opened in town. On one side of the bright
and sunny café was a wall with shelves of
plain white mugs, plates and bowls, as well
as adorable ceramic figurines shaped like
fairies, unicorns and dinosaurs. On the other
wall hung beautifully decorated ceramic
plates, the bright colours glazed and shiny.

"OK, girls," said Connie's mum. "Everyone can choose something to paint."

"How are we ever going to pick?" wondered Mia. She loved doing arts and crafts and wished she could paint everything in there!

"I'm going to paint a ballerina," said Connie, who took dance classes.

"Someone help me choose!" wailed Annabelle. She was holding a bowl in one hand, and a cute puppy figurine in the other.

"This one," said Mia, pointing at the puppy. She loved animals, so puppies got her vote every time!

Yasmina chose a big mug. "What are you

going to paint, Mia?" she asked.

"Maybe I should decorate a new water bowl for Flossy," Mia said, thinking of her pet cat. Then suddenly she spotted the perfect thing – a trinket box shaped like a heart. "Actually," she said, taking the box off the shelf. "I'm going to paint this."

As Connie's mum ordered a coffee, the girls put on aprons and sat down at a long table with jars of paint in the middle. At the table next to them, a mum and dad were holding their baby boy. They painted his feet with red paint and gently pressed them on to a plate, stamping it with his tiny footprints.

"Aw," said Annabelle. "That's so cute."

At another table, a group of grown-up ladies chatted as they decorated fruit bowls and vases with colourful patterns.

Dipping their paintbrushes into the pots of paint, Mia and her friends started painting their own items.

Yasmina painted a bright yellow tennis ball on her mug. "My dad's birthday is next week," she told the others. "I'm going to give him this as a present."

Mia drew a picture of a mermaid with long silver hair and a green tail on her trinket box.

"Ooh! That's really good," said Connie. "Are you going to keep it for yourself?"

Mia shook her head. "No," she said. "If

it turns out well I'm
going to send it to
Charlotte."

"Say hi from
us the next
time you speak
to her," said
Annabelle. The
other girls nodded.

Charlotte Williams was Mia's best friend.
She used to be in the same class as Mia and
the other girls, but not long ago Charlotte's
family had moved to America.

"Does Charlotte like California?" asked
Yasmina, now painting a purple tennis
racket on the other side of her mug.

"She loves it there," said Mia, adding delicate scales to her mermaid's tail.

"You must really miss her," said Annabelle, sympathetically. "You guys were so close."

"We still are," said Mia. Despite living thousands of miles apart, Mia and Charlotte were as close as ever. Mia bit her lip to stop herself from blurting out the amazing secret she and Charlotte shared. They still saw each other lots – at a magical place called Wishing Star Palace!

Mia and Charlotte were training to become Secret Princesses, who used magic to grant wishes. It meant they got to have exciting adventures together and help

people by doing magic!

Mia dabbed her paintbrush in bluey-green paint and started painting the bottom of the box. The turquoise paint was the exact same colour as the water in the Blue Lagoon, where Wishing Star Palace's mermaids lived. Or rather, the same colour the lagoon *used* to be. On Mia and Charlotte's last visit to Wishing Star Palace, the mermaids had been forced to leave the lagoon because of one of Princess Poison's horrible curses.

Princess Poison was the Secret Princesses' enemy. Although it was hard for Mia to believe it, Princess Poison had once been a Secret Princess. She'd been banished from the palace for using her magical powers to

help herself instead of other people. Now
instead of granting other people's wishes,
she used her magic to spoil wishes. She
was always causing trouble for the Secret
Princesses. Most recently, she'd sent a
poison frog to turn their beautiful Blue
Lagoon into a stinky green swamp!

Mia looked down at the mermaid
she'd painted and swallowed hard. The
mermaid looked just like Marina, one of
the mermaids who lived at the palace. Mia
knew that Marina and the other mermaids
must be missing their home terribly

The only way to break Princess Poison's
curse was to grant four watery wishes. Mia
and Charlotte had already granted one

– but there were still three more to go. Mia glanced down at the golden half-heart pendant on her necklace and stifled a gasp of surprise. It was glowing!

Her heart thumping so loudly she was sure her friends could hear it, Mia stood and picked up the dirty cup of water they'd been using to clean their paintbrushes. "Um, I'm just going to get some clean water," she told the others.

Mia hurried to the sink at the back of the

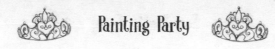
studio. Checking that nobody was looking, she held her glowing pendant tight. "I wish I could see Charlotte," she whispered.

Golden light streamed out of the pedant and swirled around Mia, lifting her into the air. Nobody even glanced up from their painting as the magic swept Mia away from

the Ceramics Café. No one would notice
she was gone, either, because time wouldn't
pass at home while Mia was off on a Secret
Princess adventure.

A moment later, Mia landed in a
beautiful room. It was full of marble pillars
and a glittering jewelled mosaic of tiaras,
hearts and stars. There were little changing
cubicles with red velvet curtains, piles of
big, fluffy white towels, and dressing tables
with hair dryers and little pots of all kinds
of gorgeous-smelling lotions. She knew
she had to be somewhere at Wishing Star
Palace, but she hadn't been in this room
before. Catching sight of herself in a full-
length mirror, Mia's blue eyes widened

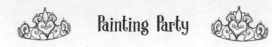
in surprise. Although a diamond tiara
had appeared on her long, blonde hair as
usual, she wasn't wearing the gorgeous
gold princess dress she normally wore at
the palace. Instead, she was wearing a gold
swimming costume with ruffles!

"Mia!" cried Charlotte, suddenly
appearing out of thin air. Like Mia, she was
wearing a swimming costume, but hers was
bright pink with a little skirt. A tiara just
like Mia's sparkled on top of her bouncy
brown curls.

"Look at these!" said Charlotte, waving
her foot in the air. "We're wearing ruby
flippers instead of ruby slippers!"

She waddled over and gave Mia a hug.

"Why do you have paint on your face?" asked Charlotte, rubbing a smudge of aquamarine paint off Mia's cheek with her thumb.

"I was at a cool new ceramics café in town with some friends from school," explained Mia. "Everyone said to say hi to you."

"Speaking of friends," said Charlotte, "where do you suppose the princesses are?"

SPLISH! SPLOSH! SPLASH!

Mia listened carefully and heard the faint sound of happy splashing coming from outside of the dressing room. She sniffed the air and caught a faint whiff of chlorine. Suddenly, she had a feeling about where they might be.

"Come on," she said, grabbing her best friend's hand. "I think the Secret Princesses might be by the pool!"

Mermaid Music

Waddling awkwardly in their jewelled red
flippers, Mia and Charlotte went outside
the changing room. They found themselves
by a swimming pool filled with sparkling
turquoise water and surrounded by palm
trees. In the distance, the white towers of
Wishing Star Palace rose up against the
blue sky, but none of the Secret Princesses

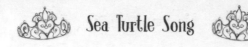
were inside the palace – they were all
around the swimming pool!

"Hi, girls!" A princess with beaded plaits
and a fringed bikini waved to them from
a sun lounger. A pendant shaped like a
thimble glittered on her necklace because
Princess Cara was a fashion designer.

A glamorous-looking princess in a sleek

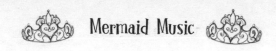
swimming costume and cool sunglasses reclined next to her. Even here at the palace, Princess Grace looked like the movie star she was back in the real world!

"We're hanging out by the pool to keep the mermaids company," explained Grace.

Since Princess Poison's frog had poisoned the Blue Lagoon's water, the four

mermaids had had to move to the palace swimming pool. Oceane, Coral, Nerida and Marina were swimming in the water, along with some of the Secret Princesses. The princesses looked like mermaids, too, because the aquamarine combs tucked into their hair had magically turned their legs into tails.

A young mermaid with pale green hair and a silver tail swam up to the side of the pool and playfully splashed the girls.

"Hi, Marina!" said Mia.

"I'm so glad you're here!" Marina squealed. "Come and play with me!"

Mia and Charlotte jumped into the pool. *SPLASH!*

"Can't catch me!" giggled Marina, her tail wiggling as she darted through the water.

Mia and Charlotte's ruby flippers helped them swim fast – but not fast enough to catch Marina!

"Not fair!" said Charlotte, panting. "We don't have mermaid tails this time."

If the girls granted three more watery wishes they wouldn't just break Princess Poison's curse – they'd earn their aquamarine combs. Then they'd be able to get mermaid tails whenever they wanted!

The girls and Marina practised handstands and somersaults in the water. After that, they sat on the bottom of the pool and pretended to have an underwater tea party.

"Want to go down the slide?" asked Charlotte when they came up to the surface. The swimming pool had a long and twisty water slide.

Marina giggled and swished her tail. "I can't climb up the ladder!"

"Oops!" said Charlotte, slapping her forehead. "Silly me!"

"I've got a game you can play!" called Princess Cara. "You can dive for treasure." She threw a gold ring into the water. It sank to the bottom and the girls dived down, racing to retrieve it.

"Got it!" cried Charlotte, rising to the surface with the ring in her hand.

As Marina and Charlotte took turns throwing the ring for each other to find, Mia floated on a cupcake-shaped inflatable.

"Taking a break?" Princess Alice asked, swimming up to her. The aquamarine comb

tucked into her strawberry-blonde hair had
given her a sparkling crimson tail.

Mia and Charlotte had known Alice for
a long time – since before she'd become
a famous pop star. When they were little,
Alice had been their babysitter. It was
Alice who had spotted the girls' potential to
become Secret Princesses.

"Guess what, Alice," said Mia. "A new
café opened in town. You can paint your
own ceramics there."

"Ooh! That sounds fun," said Princess
Alice. "I'll have to check it out the next
time I visit my parents."

"Our town must seem boring after all the
exciting places you've performed," said Mia.

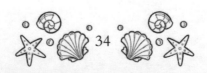

"I love going on tour," said Alice. "But it's true what they say – there's no place like home."

Mia glanced over at the mermaids. Marina was still playing with Charlotte, but Oceane, Coral and Nerida looked glum.

"The mermaids must miss their home so much," murmured Mia.

"They never complain," Alice said. "But it must be tough on them."

"I wish we could do something to help them," said Mia.

"You *are* doing something," said Alice. She touched the aquamarine sparkling in Mia's pendant. The girls had earned their first blue-green gems for granting a watery wish on their last visit to the palace. "You're breaking Princess Poison's curse."

"I know," said Mia. "But I wish we could cheer them up a bit in the meantime."

"Music always makes me feel better," Alice said. "Maybe we should sing?"

"That's a great idea!" said Mia.

Alice pulled out her aquamarine comb

and, with a shimmer, her tail transformed into legs. Climbing out of the pool, Alice waved her wand and instruments magically appeared. Strumming her guitar, she called to the others, "Let's make some music!"

Coral, a copper-haired mermaid with a purple tail, picked up a small harp and strummed along with Alice. Clicking a pair of scallop shells like castanets, Marina added a beat. Then Oceane

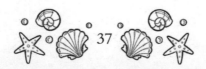

lifted a big conch shell to her lips and a
sound like a trumpet came out.

As music filled the air, Nerida, a mermaid
with a turquoise tail, began to sing. The
sweet, silvery sound was so beautiful it
gave Mia goosebumps. Soon everyone was
smiling and singing along.

"The mermaids look much happier now,"

Mia whispered to Charlotte.

"I know," Charlotte whispered back.
"But they'll be even happier once we break
Princess Poison's spell."

After they'd sung a few more songs, Mia
asked the mermaids, "Can we go and check
the Magic Pearl?"

"Of course," said Oceane. "I hope there's a
watery wish for you to grant."

Mia and Charlotte climbed out of the pool
and their ruby flippers transformed into ruby
slippers. Clicking their heels together three
times, the girls said, "The Blue Lagoon!"

Magic whisked them to a coral cave by
a lake covered in stinky green slime. An
enormous pearl lit up the cave with a glow.

As the girls got closer, they could see the image of an older girl with her long hair in a high ponytail shimmering on the pearl's surface. The girl was

wearing a sun visor and an orange T-shirt with the words *Sea Life Sanctuary* on. Mia and Charlotte touched the Magic Pearl and words appeared:

Ava's made a wish by the water so blue,
Say her name to help make it come true!

"Ava!" Mia and Charlotte called together.

Magical bubbles fizzed up around the girls and they floated away from the palace. The next thing they knew, the girls were on a hot, sunny beach with white sand. Thanks to the magic, none of the swimmers and sunbathers noticed their sudden arrival.

"I wish we still had our swimming costumes on!" Mia said, glancing down at the sundress she was now wearing.

"Do you see Ava anywhere?" asked Charlotte. There were lots of people splashing in the warm, gentle waves, but Ava didn't seem to be among them.

"She's not sunbathing," said Mia,

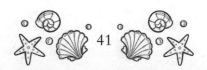

scanning towels and blankets on the sand.

"Wait a minute," said Charlotte, spotting a familiar orange T-shirt. "Isn't that her?"

Ava crouched down, picked something up, and put it in the black bin bag she was carrying.

"Let's go help her," said Mia. She picked up a plastic bottle, then ran over to Ava and dropped it in her bin bag.

"Thanks," said Ava, smiling at her gratefully. "I'm Ava."

"I'm Charlotte, and this is Mia," said Charlotte, smiling back.

"Do you work at the Sea Life Sanctuary?" asked Mia.

"Yes," Ava said proudly. "I'm a volunteer."

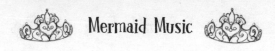

"So why are you picking up rubbish?" asked Charlotte.

"Litter is really bad for marine life," explained Ava. "Especially at this time of year. Baby sea turtles are going to hatch on this beach soon – maybe even tonight!"

"Wow!" said Mia. "That's so cool!"

"Sea turtles are endangered," said Ava.

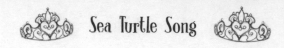

"So I'm doing everything I can to help. I really wish the hatching goes well and the baby turtles make it to the sea safely."

"We'd love to help you," said Charlotte, picking up a crisp packet and adding it to Ava's bag.

"And the sea turtles," said Mia. *The mermaids, too!* she added silently. Because if they granted Ava's wish, Mia and Charlotte would be one step closer to breaking Princess Poison's curse!

CHAPTER THREE

Beach Buddies

Mia and Charlotte walked along the water's
edge with Ava. The wet sand was dotted
with delicate white sand dollars, fan-shaped
cockle shells and bumpy starfish. Sadly, as
well as the beautiful seashells, there was
also lots of litter. Every time they spotted a
bit of rubbish the girls stopped and put it in
Ava's bin bag.

"I never realised how much litter you get on beaches," said Mia.

"I know," said Charlotte. "It's really sad."

"Where are the sea turtles' nests?" asked Mia, looking around. She couldn't see any nests on the beach.

"They're buried under the warm sand near the dunes," explained Ava. "About two months ago, hundreds of sea turtle mums came out of the water and dug holes with their flippers to lay their eggs. They always return to the same beach where they were born."

"That's so cool," said Charlotte.

Ava nodded. "But it's even cooler to see the babies hatching! I've never seen it, but

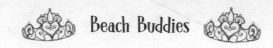

I've heard all about it from my friends at the sanctuary."

"I'd love to see that," said Mia.

Picking up a chocolate bar wrapper, Ava sighed. "But so many things can go wrong," she said. "That's why I'm trying to keep the beach clean – to

make it as safe as possible for the baby turtles. It's so important for them to survive because sea turtles are so endangered."

"What does endangered mean?" asked Charlotte.

"It means they're at risk of dying out,"
said Ava, her voice trembling slightly.

Mia squeezed Ava's arm sympathetically.
It made her really sad to think of a world
without sea turtles, too.

"But why are sea turtles endangered?"
asked Charlotte.

"Lots of reasons," said Ava, clearing her
throat. "Pollution is a big problem. When
chemicals or oil get into the water it makes
the turtles ill. Another reason is that people
have built houses and hotels on the beaches
where sea turtles nest."

A plastic bag washed up on to the beach
and Charlotte picked it up.

"Plastic bags like those are really, really

48

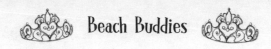

bad for sea turtles," said Ava.

"Really?" said Charlotte. "Why?"

"Because they look like jellyfish," explained Ava, "and sea turtles eat jellyfish. When they swallow plastic bags by mistake it hurts their tummies."

"You know so much about animals," Mia said to Ava, impressed.

"I want to be a marine biologist when I grow up," said Ava. "That's why I'm volunteering at the Sea Life Sanctuary – so I can learn as much as possible about marine life."

"I bet you don't know the answer to this, though," said Charlotte. "Why don't oysters share their pearls?"

Ava looked puzzled. "Huh?"

Charlotte grinned and held up an oyster shell. "Because they're *shellfish*. Get it?"

Ava laughed out loud at Charlotte's joke. "I'll have to tell that to the others back at the sanctuary," she said, pointing to the big building at the end of the beach.

A bit further along, Mia spotted the clear plastic rings from a six-pack of drinks washing up on shore. She fished the object out of the foamy water.

"These are really dangerous, too," said Ava. "Not just for sea turtles – but for birds as well. They can get them caught around their necks."

Shuddering at the thought, Mia dropped

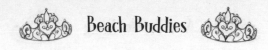

the litter into Ava's bin bag.

Ava fished them out and broke the rings up. "You should always break those plastic rings up before recycling them," said Ava.

"I'll definitely do that from now on," Mia promised.

"Me too," agreed Charlotte. "I just never thought about litter hurting sea creatures."

"The sanctuary tries to teach people about protecting marine life," said Ava. "But it costs a lot to look after injured animals so there's not a lot of money left over to get the message out."

"Well, I've got a big mouth," said Charlotte, grinning. "So I'm going to tell everyone I know not to litter!"

"So am I," said Mia.

Nearby, a family with young children was getting ready to leave the beach. Mia was happy to see that they weren't just packing up their towels and toys – they were taking their rubbish away too!

"Too bad not everyone remembers to take their rubbish home," said Ava, holding

up a plastic straw. "These drive me nuts.
If straws get washed out to sea, they get
stuck up turtles' noses and stop them from
breathing."

Mia's eyes misted with tears at the
thought.

When the
rubbish bag was
full, Ava went to
put it in a rubbish
bin. While they
were waiting for
her to come back,
the girls slipped
off their flip-flops
and waded into

the water to paddle. Sunlight danced on the waves, making the water glitter like the aquamarines on the girls' pendants.

"Ouh! It's lovely," said Charlotte, as the water lapped over her toes.

"I wish we could go for a swim," said Mia.

"I can't wait to get our aquamarine combs," said Charlotte. "Then we can get mermaid tails and go swimming whenever we like."

"Marina would love it here," Mia said quietly, watching children jumping in the water and riding the waves on boogie boards.

Charlotte squeeze her hand. "Don't worry, Mia," she said. "We're going to find a

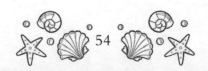

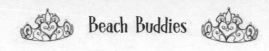
way to grant Ava's wish,"

"I know we will," said Mia. The mermaids were counting on them. Letting them down was not an option!

CHUG CHUG CHUG CHUG!

A noisy engine drowned out the sound of seagulls squawking and children splashing. A big boat was speeding towards the beach.

"Hey!" shouted Ava, running down to the water's edge. She waved her hand wildly in the air, trying to get the captain's attention. "Stay on the other side of the buoys!"

"What's wrong?" Mia asked her.

"Boats aren't supposed to come so close to the shore during the turtle nesting season," explained Ava.

"Go away!" Mia and Charlotte yelled, jumping up and down. "You're too close to the beach!"

The captain stepped on to the deck and waved at them.

"Phew!" said Ava. "He's seen us."

But instead of turning the boat around and sailing back out to sea, the captain

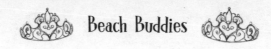

rolled a plastic barrel along the deck. It had a skull and crossbones stamped on its side and the words "Toxic Waste" in big letters. Tipping the barrel over the side of the boat, he poured the contents into the water.

"What's he doing?" gasped Ava, watching in horror as the captain tipped another barrel into the water.

"Yikes!" cried Mia, jumping back as the waves washed sludgy green waste on to the beach.

As the short, tubby captain dumped barrel after barrel into the water, Charlotte said, "I know who that is."

"Me too," said Mia grimly. Even from a distance she recognised Hex – Princess Poison's horrible assistant! He grinned at them triumphantly.

Shouts of "Ew!" and "Yuck!" rang out across the beach as people leapt out of the water to avoid the green sludge.

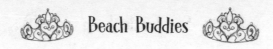

"This is a disaster," said Ava as the goo spilled on to the sand. "There's no way we can get all this mess cleaned up before the sea turtles hatch."

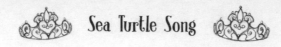

Mia and Charlotte exchanged looks. "Oh yes, there is," said Charlotte.

Mia nodded and held her pendant out towards Charlotte's. It was time for the girls to make a wish!

CHAPTER FOUR
Sea Life Sanctuary

Mia and Charlotte put their pendants together, making a glowing gold heart.

"I wish to clean the beach up," said Charlotte.

There was flash of golden light and instantly the toxic waste disappeared. Not a drop remained in the water or on the powdery sand.

Hex shook his fist at them, then stormed into the boat's cabin. A moment later the boat revved its engine, spun around and sailed out to sea.

"Good riddance!" Charlotte shouted as the boat zoomed away.

"Thank you so much!" Ava said, overjoyed. "That was the coolest thing ever."

The swimmers had run back into the water as if nothing strange had happened. Ava stared at them splashing in the waves.

"Why isn't anyone else amazed?" Ava asked. "Did I just imagine that you cleaned up the spill?" She squinted up at the sunny sky. "It's pretty hot today. Maybe I have

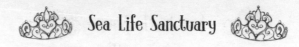
heatstroke or something ..."

"You definitely don't have heatstroke,"
Mia reassured Ava.

"So that really happened?" Ava said.

"Yup," said Charlotte. "It was magic – but
you're the only one who noticed."

"It's because we're training to become

Secret Princesses," explained Mia. "We can use magic to help grant your wish for the sea turtles to hatch safely."

"That's wonderful," said Ava, her face lighting up. "The turtles need all the help they can get!"

"Sometimes the people we help find it hard to believe in magic," Charlotte told Ava. "But not you."

"Nature makes it easy for me to believe in magic," said Ava. "Living things are always blowing my mind. For instance, how do sea turtles know to return to the exact spot where they were born? It might not be magic – but it is pretty incredible."

Mia smiled at Ava. "I think so too."

"Do you two want to come and have a look around the Sea Life Sanctuary?" Ava asked them.

Mia and Charlotte grinned at each other. "Yes please!" they shouted in unison.

Ava led them to a long building jutting into the water. There was a sea turtle sculpture made out of recycled metal outside the building.

"The sanctuary mostly helps sea turtles," said Ava, "but it looks after other local marine life, too."

Staff members in orange T-shirts like Ava's waved to the girls as they went inside.

"Hi, everyone!" Ava called. "I'm giving my friends Mia and Charlotte a tour."

"Welcome!" said a lady with a long grey plait. She was holding a bucket of crabs in one hand and a bucket of seaweed in the other. "I'm Steph, a marine biologist here. Do you want to help me feed the sea turtles?"

Mia and Charlotte nodded eagerly.

Steph took them to a big tank with two enormous turtles swimming in it.

"Oh my goodness!" exclaimed Charlotte. "They're bigger than I am!"

"They're gorgeous," said Mia.

"This is Sammy," said Ava, pointing to the bigger turtle, with a bumpy reddish-brown shell. "He's a loggerhead turtle. He had plastic stuck in his tummy but we gave

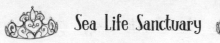

him an operation and he's recovering well."

"He's just starting to get his appetite back," said Steph. She let Charlotte tip the bucket of crabs into the tank.

"I thought you said that sea turtles ate jellyfish," said Mia.

"Lots do," said Ava. "But loggerhead

turtles have really strong jaws, so they can eat things with hard shells – like crabs."

"Olive is a green turtle," said Steph, pointing to the slightly smaller turtle. Her dark green shell had a long jagged crack across it. "She mostly eats seaweed and seagrass." She handed Mia the second bucket. "Why don't you give her some now?"

As she tipped the bucket of seaweed into the water, Mia asked, "What happened to Olive's shell?"

"We're not sure," said Ava. "The wound might have been caused by a boat's propeller."

"Shell wounds are always really serious,"

said Steph, "because a turtle's shell protects all their internal organs."

"Luckily Olive's doing a lot better now," said Ava. "We'll be releasing her back into the ocean soon."

Steph showed them a small electronic device stuck to Olive's shell. "This will let us track Olive once she goes back to the sea. We'll keep an eye on how she's doing and learn more about sea turtle behaviour."

When they had finished feeding the turtles, Ava showed them the intensive care unit where special marine vets treated the sickest animals. The girls couldn't go inside, but they could peek inside through the big glass windows.

A vet in a white coat was carefully bandaging a bird with a very long beak.

"That's a pelican," said Ava. "It got a fishing hook stuck in its leg."

"Ouch!" said Charlotte, wincing in sympathy.

"Fishing equipment is a big threat to marine life," said Ava. "We help a lot of animals that get tangled up in fishing lines and nets."

Next Ava took them to a big tank that was half inside the building and half outside. A huge grey creature swam up to the side of the tank, pressing its nose against the glass. One of its flippers was missing.

"Oh my gosh!" gasped Mia. "It's a manatee! I've always wanted to see one."

"Lots live in the warm, shallow water around here," Ava said. "But they often get injured by boats, like Martha, because manatees swim really slowly."

71

"Hi, Martha," said Charlotte, reaching out and touching the glass.

Martha rose up to the surface, her smooth back and whiskery snout sticking out of the water.

"Can I stroke her?" asked Mia, desperate to touch the manatee.

Ava shook her head. "No, we're not allowed."

"Does she bite?" asked Charlotte.

"Oh no," said Ava, laughing. "Manatees are really gentle. But Martha's going to be released soon, so it's really important that she doesn't get too used to humans or she won't be able to adjust to being back out in the wild."

"Good luck, gorgeous girl," said Mia, waving goodbye to the manatee.

"I've saved the best for last," said Ava, grinning.

She led them to a room at the end of a corridor. A blast of cold air hit Mia's face when Ava opened the door.

Sleek black and white birds were swimming in a pool of water and waddling around the surrounding rocks.

"Penguins!" squealed Mia.

"But don't penguins only live in cold places?" asked Charlotte.

"Actually," said Ava, "some penguins do live in warm places – like the Galapagos penguin. But these little guys prefer

cold climates. They're only living here
temporarily. The zoo they live at was hit
by a hurricane and their enclosure got
damaged, so they're staying with us until
it's fixed."

"They are so cute!" cooed Mia, watching
as a penguin slid on its tummy down a rock

and splashed into the water.

"He's got a Mohican haircut," giggled Charlotte, pointing at a penguin with a funny tuft of feathers on its head. Charlotte waddled around the room, her hands stuck out by her sides, imitating the punky penguin's walk.

"That's a rockhopper penguin," said Ava.

RIBBIT!

The girls turned around and saw a familiar fat green frog, its eyes bulging and its throat puffed out.

"Hey!" said Ava,

frowning. "How did you get in here?"

The frog started hopping towards the penguins' pool.

"It must have escaped from another part of the sanctuary," said Ava. She moved towards the frog to catch it.

"Stop, Ava!" shouted Mia. "You can't touch it!"

"It's poisonous!" cried Charlotte.

"How do you know?" asked Ava, puzzled.

"Just trust us," said Mia. There was no time to explain that the frog was Toxin, Princess Poison's pet.

Croaking loudly, Toxin bounded across the room and jumped on top of the thermostat up on the wall. Then he reached

forward and twiddled the temperature
control dial with his webbed toes.

"Hey! Don't touch that!" shouted Ava.
"The water needs to be cold."

Green slime dripping from his toes, Toxin

turned the thermostat up high.

As the temperature rose, the room suddenly started to feel warmer.

"Oh no!" wailed Ava. "The penguins are going to overheat!"

CHAPTER FIVE
Pass the Mayo!

The penguin room was getting hotter and hotter. Charlotte's cheeks were flushed from the heat and Mia was starting to sweat. The poor penguins waddled out of the hot water, shaking their black and white feathers in distress.

"We've got to lower the temperature," said Mia.

"We can't touch the dial!" said Charlotte. "Toxin's covered it in poison."

There was only one thing to do.

Mia and Charlotte held their necklaces together.

"I wish for the perfect penguin enclosure," said Mia.

Magical light flashed out of their pendants and the room was chilly once more. Now a big, smooth iceberg rose out of the water. Over by the rocks, a cosy igloo had also appeared.

WHEE! Honking and squawking, penguins slid down the iceberg on their bellies and shot into the water. They glided through the chilly water, their flippers

held gracefully by
their sides. Grown-
up penguins huddled
inside the igloo with
their fluffy chicks,
while other penguins
stood on top of
it, preening their

glistening black feathers.

"They're having so much fun!" said Ava happily.

But Toxin didn't seem to be enjoying the cold as much as the penguins. Shivering, the frog bounded away.

"Don't come back unless you want to end up on the endangered species list!" Charlotte shouted after him.

"What type of frog was that?" Ava asked her. "I know a lot about animals, but I've never heard of frog that can poison water."

"It's a magic frog," said Mia. "It belongs to someone called Princess Poison."

Before the girls could explain further, Steph popped her head around the door.

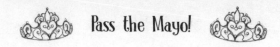

"Someone's just brought in a hawksbill turtle. It's in a really bad way," she said. "Can you three give me a hand?"

"Of course," said Ava.

The girls followed Steph to a room where a turtle was lying on an examining table. It was much smaller than the other turtles

at the sanctuary and its shell was almost completely covered in sticky black tar.

"Poor thing!" said Mia.

"What happened to it?" asked Charlotte.

"It must have got caught up in an oil spill," said Steph. "Oil floats on the water's surface, and when sea turtles come up to breathe they get covered in it."

The marine biologist gave the girls plastic gloves to put on. Then she got out paper towels and a big jar of mayonnaise.

"Are you going to make a sandwich?" asked Charlotte.

"No," Steph said, chuckling. "We're going to use it to clean the shell."

Steph gently coated the turtle's shell with

the white spread. "Mayonnaise sticks to the oil," she explained. "It makes it much easier to clean it off." She wiped the mayo away with a paper towel and the black tar came off too, revealing a bit of the turtle's shell.

The girls carefully helped Steph clean off the tar. Then Steph spooned some mayonnaise mixed with cod liver oil into the turtle's mouth.

"Do turtles like mayonnaise?" asked Mia.

"Not really," said Steph. "But the mayo will bind with any oil

that the turtle swallowed and help it come out the other end."

"Ew!" said Charlotte, wrinkling her nose.

"Better out than in," said Steph, grinning. "Otherwise the oil will make the turtle ill."

Once all of the sticky black oil had been scrubbed off, Mia saw that the hawksbill's shell was gorgeous. It had overlapping scales with beautiful orangey-brown patterns.

"What a pretty shell," said Mia.

"It's what's made hawksbill turtles so rare," said Ava sadly. "People hunted them for their shells."

"Fortunately this one's going to be fine," said Steph, stroking the turtle's shell. "Are

you heading home now, Ava?"

"I might hang out on the beach for a while," said Ava. "In case tonight's the night the turtles hatch."

"Can we come too?" asked Charlotte.

"Of course," replied Ava.

A worrying thought suddenly occurred to Mia. What if the turtles didn't hatch tonight while they were there to help?

"Thanks, girls," said Steph, waving them goodbye. "This little dude will be back home in the ocean before he knows it."

But what about the mermaids? thought Mia. Would they be back home soon too? It all depended on whether she and Charlotte could grant Ava's wish.

87

Outside, night had fallen and the sky was dark. Inky water shimmered in the glow of a full moon. Everyone had gone home and the only sound was the waves lapping gently against the sand.

As they walked along the empty beach, Ava said, "I've been coming down here

every night for the past week. I really hope tonight's the night."

"So do I," Mia whispered to Charlotte. "If the turtles don't hatch tonight, how are we going to grant Ava's wish?"

"I was wondering that too," Charlotte whispered back. "Maybe we'll have to come back?"

"The loggerheads made their nests around here," said Ava quietly, sitting down by the sand dunes. "Did you know that each turtle lays around a hundred eggs – each one the size of a ping pong ball?"

"Wow!" said Charlotte.

"We need to be really quiet," whispered Ava, putting her finger to her lips.

89

"Scientists say that turtle hatchlings actually talk to each other from inside their eggs. That's how they all know to hatch at the same time. It's safer for them to all be together."

Ava pointed up at the sky. "I'm glad it's a full moon," she said in a hushed tone. "Bright moonlight guides the hatchlings out to the sea. That's why I didn't bring a torch – any other light confuses them and they could go in the wrong direction."

Mia quickly tucked her necklace into her sundress. The pendant was glowing very faintly, because there was only enough magic left for one more wish, but Mia didn't want to confuse the turtle hatchlings!

The girls sat in silence for a while, watching the sand hopefully. Suddenly a flash of blue lit up the dark.

"Where's that light coming from?" asked Ava.

Mia looked down at her hand and gasped. Her sapphire ring was flashing and so was Charlotte's. It could only mean one thing – danger was near!

"Fancy meeting you girls here!" shrieked a loud voice.

Mia looked up and saw a tall woman in green striding down the beach. Her long hair was as black as the night sky, except for a streak of white.

"Can you please keep your voice down," Ava said softly. "Sea turtles might be hatching tonight."

"Oh, goodie!" boomed Princess Poison even louder. "I was hoping to see some ickle bitty sea turtles. I just *love* animals." She smirked at the girls. "Especially frogs." Princess Poison laughed meanly.

Mia and Charlotte glared at her.

"Go away, Princess Poison," Charlotte

told her. "Your nasty frog couldn't stop us, and you won't be able to either."

"Well, if frogs don't work, I'll just have to try some other creature," said Princess Poison.

She pointed her wand at the water and hissed a spell:

Into the dark cast magic green sparks,
And fill the water with circling sharks!

A shower of green sparks flew out of Princess Poison's wand, landing on the water.

"Oh no!" cried Mia, covering her mouth in horror. Everywhere the sparks had fallen,

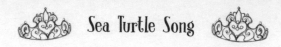

pointy dorsal fins were now sticking out of
the water. If the sea turtles went into the
water, they were going to get eaten!

CHAPTER SIX
Hatching a Plan

"What have you done?" cried Ava. "The sharks will eat the baby sea turtles!"

"Nature can be harsh," said Princess Poison, smirking. "Just like me." Then, waving her wand, Princess Poison vanished in a blaze of green light.

"Please do something," Ava begged the girls. "Hatchlings are so tiny. They don't

stand a chance against sharks."

"It's OK," Mia told Ava. "We'll make another wish." She held her pendant against Charlotte's. The faint glow from the heart was just bright enough for her to see the worry on her best friend's face.

"What should we wish for?" Charlotte asked. This was their last wish – it was important to get it right.

"I know," said Mia. "I wish for the the sharks to become stars!"

The sharks instantly vanished from the water. Overhead, the sky twinkled with stars that had magically appeared. Gazing up, Mia thought that she could make out the shape of a shark in the night sky.

"Look, Charlotte!" she whispered, tracing the dorsal fin with her finger.

"There's a constellation called the Great Bear," said Charlotte. "And now there's a Great White too!"

"That was a brilliant idea!" said Ava.

"Now there's even more light to guide the hatchlings to the sea."

"Why do the turtles hatch at night anyway?" asked Charlotte quietly. "Wouldn't they see better in daylight?"

"Well, there are two reasons," said Ava. "First, it's safer at night when there are fewer predators on the beach. Also because when the sun sets, the sand cools down."

"That makes sense," said Charlotte, nodding.

"Now I've got a question for you," said Ava. "What was the deal with that lady?"

"That was Princess Poison," said Mia. "It was her frog that made the penguins' water too hot back at the sanctuary."

"The guy who dumped the toxic waste in the sea works for her too," said Charlotte.

"Why are they doing this?" asked Ava. "What do they have against sea turtles?"

"It's not really about the sea turtles," explained Mia. "Princess Poison is trying to spoil your wish because it makes her more powerful."

"Oh," said Ava, looking upset. "I hate that she's putting the turtles at risk."

"Me too," said Mia, squeezing Ava's shoulder sympathetically. "But don't worry – we'll be doing everything we can to stop her."

As they sat in silence, watching the sand, Mia heard a faint rustling noise.

"Do you hear that?" she whispered.

Charlotte nodded, her brown eyes shining with excitement.

Just beyond where they were sitting, the sand was shifting. Something was trying to emerge!

"It's happening!" whispered Ava. "The hatchlings are digging their way out!"

They watched in awe as tiny turtle heads poked out of the sand.

"Let's give them a hand," Ava said softly. The girls carefully brushed sand away, revealing hundreds of wriggling baby turtles. The hatchlings climbed on top of each other in their rush to scramble out of the hole.

"Oh my gosh," Mia breathed. "They are so tiny."

"The turtles are over here!" bellowed a man's voice, interrupting the moment.

Princess Poison and Hex, holding bright torches, were leading a big group of people along the beach.

"I'm so excited!" squealed an older lady with a fancy camera around her neck.

"This is definitely the highlight of my holiday," said a man wearing a tropical-print shirt and holding a torch.

"This is, like, totally amazing," said a teenaged girl, who was using her mobile phone as a torch.

The tourists crowded around the nest and peered down at the wriggling hatchlings.

"They're adorable!" exclaimed the lady. She snapped photos with her camera, the flash lighting up the dark.

The man aimed the beam of his torch right at the hole. "Just look at those little critters go," he said.

SNAP! SNAP! SNAP! The teenager used her phone to take pictures. "I can't wait to show these to my friends," she said.

The tourists cheered loudly as the first turtles made their way out of the hole.

"Ssh!" said Ava, putting her finger to her lips. But everyone ignored her.

"Please make another wish," Ava begged Mia and Charlotte. Her eyes were wild with worry. "The noise is going to confuse the hatchlings. They need

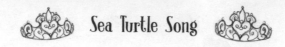
to be able to hear the waves or they won't be able to find their way to the sea."

"We can't," said Charlotte. "We only get to make three wishes and we've used them up already."

"Let's sing *Happy Birthday* to the turtles," said Princess Poison, "since they're being born today."

The tourists began to sing enthusiastically:

Happy Birthday to you, Happy Birthday to you …

More and more sea turtles spilled out of the hole, as the tourists sang and snapped photos. But instead of crawling towards the water, the sea turtles started heading inland.

"Oh no," wailed Ava in dismay. "They're ▪▪ing the wrong way."

Happy Birthday, dear turtles—

"Stop!" shouted Mia.

"What's wrong?" said Princess Poison, putting her hands on her hips. "Don't you want to celebrate the turtles being born?"

"Of course I want to celebrate," said Mia. "But not by making lots of noise."

"The noise and light is confusing the hatchlings," said Charlotte.

"You're just being party poopers," said Princess Poison.

"Party poopers! Party poopers!" Hex jeered loudly.

"They aren't being party poopers," said Ava. "I volunteer at the Sea Life Sanctuary. Everything they said is right. The turtles need to be able to see the moonlight and hear the waves to find their way to the sea."

"Nonsense," sneered Princess Poison. "We have every right to be on the beach. You can't tell us what to do." Her green eyes

glittering, she walked up to Mia and hissed in her ear, "And you two don't have any magic left to stop me."

Maybe we don't need magic, thought Mia.

Taking a deep breath, Mia summoned up all her courage and spoke to the crowd. "Sea turtles are an endangered species," she told the tourists. "It's our responsibility to protect them. I love animals and I can tell you do too," she continued,

her voice steady even though there were butterflies in her tummy. "So will you help these hatchlings make it into the water safely?"

"Ignore her," said Princess Poison. "She's just being a spoilsport. The turtles know what to do."

"Please," Charlotte begged the crowd. "My friend's right. Will you help the turtles?"

Mia bit her lip anxiously. Had they managed to convince everyone?

CHAPTER SEVEN

Making a Splash

Mia, Charlotte and Ava waited with bated breath as the baby sea turtles scrabbled around in all directions.

"The girls are right," said the lady with the camera. "The hatchlings don't know where to go. We need to help them."

The man in the tropical-print shirt nodded. "What can we do?"

A smile of relief spread across Ava's face. "Let's make a clear path to the sea for the turtles," she said.

Everyone – except Princess Poison and Hex – got down on their knees and brushed the sand with their hands, making a smooth path leading down to the sea.

"You were really brave," Charlotte whispered to Mia as they worked. "I know you don't like talking in front of people."

"Thanks," murmured Mia.

"This is totally unnecessary," huffed Princess Poison.

"No, it's not," said Ava. "Even a footprint or a piece of driftwood is a huge obstacle for a tiny baby turtle."

Hex kicked the sand in annoyance, messing up the path.

"Stop that!" said the teenaged girl, quickly smoothing the sand down again.

"We want to help the sea turtles," said the lady with the camera, "not hurt them."

"You should leave if you aren't going to help!" said the man with the tropical-print shirt.

"Come along, Hex," ordered Princess Poison.

"This is a waste of time." They stomped off down the beach.

"And don't come back," muttered Charlotte.

When the path led all the way down to the water, Ava said, "Now let's build up the sides with sand."

The tourists lined either side of the path, quickly patting the edges into low walls so the hatchlings couldn't crawl off in the wrong direction.

When they were done, everyone watched in happy silence as the turtle hatchlings crawled down the sandy path. Their progress was slow, but thanks to the path, none of them got stuck or went the wrong

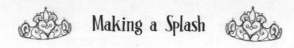

way. As the first few turtles reached the surf, they dived into the water and got swept out to sea. Mia could see moonlight glinting off bobbing turtle shells as the hatchlings frantically paddled their flippers. More and more hatchlings dived into the waves until

every last one had entered the water.

"Yay!" everyone cheered. "They made it!"

"Thank you so much for your help," said Ava. "Now the hatchlings are going to swim for two whole days without stopping. They want to get to deep water, where they'll be safer. They won't come back to this beach until they're grown up and ready to lay eggs themselves."

The lady with the camera dabbed her eyes. "That was the most beautiful thing I've ever seen."

Mia smiled at her. She felt exactly the same way!

"If you want to find out more about sea turtles, come and visit the Sea Life

Sanctuary tomorrow," said Ava.

"We will," promised the man in the tropical print shirt.

Ava hugged Mia and Charlotte. "Thank you so much. The sea turtles hatched safely," she said. "You two made my wish come true!"

Another person suddenly appeared next to them, holding a guitar. Thanks to the magic, only Mia, Charlotte and Ava noticed her sudden arrival.

"Hi, girls," Princess Alice said, beaming at them. "Well done for helping the sea turtles."

"Are you Alice de Silver?" asked Ava, her eyes wide with amazement.

"The one and only," said Alice, winking. "Do you want to hear a song I wrote? It's inspired by the three of you."

As Alice started to strum her guitar, the tourists gathered around.

"Oh my goodness!" gasped a lady. "Is it really her?"

But when Alice started to sing there was no doubting that it was really Alice de Silver – the famous pop star. People pulled out their phones and started to video Alice's surprise performance.

Sing for the turtles, swimming in the sea,
Their future depends on you and me.
The ocean is deep and aquamarine,
It's home to the turtles, so keep it clean!

"I can't wait to share this video online!" said the lady with the camera.

"I just did!" said the teenaged girl. "I've got hundreds of likes already!"

Alice winked at Mia and Charlotte. "That's exactly what I hoped would happen. It will help get the message out about protecting sea turtles."

"This is so great," said Ava.

"Glad to help," said Alice. "Now would you mind if the girls and I sneak away? We're old friends and we have a lot to catch up on."

"Of course not," said Ava. Waving goodbye she said, "I'll never forget this magical night."

"Neither will we," said Mia.

Alice put an arm around each of the girls and steered them down the beach, away from the crowd.

"Well done, girls," said Alice. "You granted another watery wish." She took out her magic wand and tapped Mia's necklace.

A second aquamarine appeared in the
pedant, sparkling in the moonlight. Then
Alice tapped Charlotte's pendant, giving
her a second gem too.

"We're halfway to breaking Princess
Poison's curse now," said Charlotte. "Only
two more wishes to grant and we'll fix the
Blue Lagoon."

"And get your aquamarine combs," Alice
reminded them.

"How are the mermaids doing?" Mia asked
Alice.

"They're really proud of you," said Alice.
"They were delighted that the sea turtles
hatched safely."

"It was incredible," said Mia.

Alice smiled. "Sometimes nature is the most magical thing of all."

"But I love doing magic," Charlotte said. "I hope we get to grant another watery wish soon."

"I'm sure you will," said Alice.

"See you soon," Charlotte said, hugging Mia goodbye.

"Look out for something in the post," said Mia with a smile.

"Oooh, what is it?" Charlotte asked. "Give me a hint."

"You'll just have to wait and see," said Mia mysteriously, her eyes twinkling.

Alice waved her wand and the magic sent the girls home. Seconds later Mia found

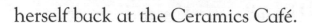
herself back at the Ceramics Café.

Taking a cup of clean water back to the
table, she sat down with her friends and
resumed painting her trinket box.

"That's so pretty," said Yasmina.
"Charlotte's going to love it. She can keep
all her jewellery inside."

Painting a green sea turtle next to the
mermaid, Mia smiled to herself. She knew
one piece of jewellery Charlotte wouldn't be
putting the box – her magic wish necklace.
The girls never took them off. After all, how
else would they know when they were about
to have another wonderful Secret Princess
adventure!

The End

Join Charlotte and Mia in their next
Secret Princesses adventure,

Seaside Fun

read on for a sneak peek!

"Yum," said Charlotte Williams, helping
herself to a still-warm orange and cranberry
muffin. She and her family were having
breakfast on their sunny patio.

Charlotte took a big bite of muffin. "These
are delicious, Dad," she said.

"Thanks," said Dad. "I used the oranges
from our trees."

Back in England, Charlotte's family had had apple trees in their garden. But here in California, where they had moved not long ago, there were orange trees in their yard. Dad was always thinking up new recipes to use up the fruit.

"What are we doing today?" asked Liam, Charlotte's little brother.

"Can we go to the beach?" said Harvey, Liam's twin.

Charlotte nodded eagerly, her mouth too full of muffin to speak.

"The surf conditions are supposed to be great today," said Dad.

"What about your homework?" said Mum, sipping freshly squeezed orange juice.

"We finished it yesterday after school," said Harvey.

"The beach sounds great," said Mum. "But we need to get all our weekend chores done first."

Liam and Harvey groaned as Mum pulled out a to-do list.

"What should we do first?" Charlotte asked helpfully. She knew that the sooner they got their chores done, the sooner they'd all be riding the waves!

Studying her list, Mum said, "I'll mow the lawn, your dad can vacuum, and you kids can wash the car."

After clearing the breakfast things away, Charlotte and her brothers went into the garage to fetch a bucket and three big sponges. Charlotte filled the bucket up with water from the hose and added special soap, sloshing it around to make the water bubbly.

Dipping their sponges in the sudsy water, Charlotte and her brothers soaped the car.

"You two should give yourselves a wash while you're at it," Charlotte teased. "You're beginning to pong."

Read *Seaside Fun* to find out what happens next!

Saving Our Oceans

Sea turtles, and many other sea creatures, are endangered. There are lots of things you can do to help protect the amazing animals that live in our oceans.

1. Don't litter! Rubbish can be hazardous to birds and other animals and pollutes our oceans.

2. Use a refillable water bottle. Plastic stays around for hundreds of years. Instead of buying disposable plastic water bottles, refill a reusable bottle.

3. Always use a reusable bag instead of plastic bags.

4. Use less energy. By turning off lights and using less water you can help reduce global warming, which is making the oceans warmer.

5. Don't release balloons. They look pretty floating in the air, but once they pop sea turtles and other animals can swallow them.

6. Share these tips with your friends!

Fun Sea Turtle Facts

• Sea turtles can get very old. The biggest species can live for up to 80 years!

• Leatherback sea turtles are huge. They can weigh up to 450kg!

• Sea turtles have been on earth for over 100 million years. They were around at the same time as the dinosaurs!

• Sea turtles travel long distances to feed, sometimes crossing entire oceans.

• Six out of the seven species of sea turtle are threatened or endangered.

• Male sea turtles spend their entire life at sea, but adult females come to shore to lay their eggs every 2–5 years. A female sea turtle can lay up to 180 eggs in a single nesting season!

• Sea turtles live in the ocean but they need air to breathe.

• Sea turtles eat everything from seaweed to jellyfish, depending on the species. Some turtles eat squid, sponges and sea anemones, while others eat only seagrass and algae.

• Leatherback sea turtles do not have hard shells. Their shells soft and leathery, just as t¹ name suggests.

Secret PRINCESSES

What would you wish for?

Are you a Secret Princess?

Join the Secret Princesses Club at:

secretprincessesbooks.co.uk

Explore the magic of the
Secret Princesses and discover:

♥ Special competitions! ♥
♥ Exclusive content! ♥
♥ All the latest princess news! ♥